A Girl's Best Friend

by Catherine Stine

illustrated by Arcana Studios

⭐ American Girl®

Questions or comments? Call 1-800-845-0005, visit our Web site at
americangirl.com, or write to Customer Service, American Girl,
8400 Fairway Place, Middleton, WI 53562-0497.

Printed in China
10 11 12 13 14 15 LEO 10 9 8 7 6 5 4 3 2 1

Illustrated by Thu Thai at Arcana Studios

Special thanks to Dr. Sandra Sawchuk, DVM

Cataloging-in-Publication Data available from the Library of Congress.

Welcome to Innerstar University! At this imaginary, one-of-a-kind school, you can live with your friends in a dorm called Brightstar House and find lots of fun ways to let your true talents shine. Your friends at Innerstar U will help you find your way through some challenging situations, too.

When you reach a page in this book that asks you to make a decision, choose carefully. The decisions you make will lead to more than 20 different endings! (*Hint:* Use a pencil to check off your choices. That way, you'll never read the same story twice.)

Want to try another ending? Read the book again—and then again. Find out what would have happened if you'd made *different* choices. Then head to www.innerstarU.com for even more book endings, games, and fun with friends.

Innerstar Guides

Every girl needs a few good friends to help her find her way. These are the friends who are always there for **you.**

Emmy

A brave girl who loves swimming and boating

Isabel

A confident girl with a funky sense of style

Riley

A good sport, on the field and off

Paige

A nature lover who leads hikes and campus cleanups

Amber

An animal lover and
a loyal friend

Neely

A creative girl who loves
dance, music, and art

Logan

A super-smart girl
who is curious about
EVERYTHING

Shelby

A kind girl who is there
for her friends—and loves
making NEW friends!

Innerstar U Campus

1. Rising Star Stables
2. Star Student Center
3. Brightstar House
4. Starlight Library
5. Sparkle Studios
6. Blue Sky Nature Center

7. Real Spirit Center
8. Five-Points Plaza
9. Starfire Lake & Boathouse
10. U-Shine Hall
11. Good Sports Center
12. Shopping Square
13. The Market
14. Morningstar Meadow

[I] t's puppy time!" you say, nudging your friend Isabel. You're on your way to Pet-Palooza, a daycare center for animals. You and Isabel just graduated from a pet-sitting course, so you can finally volunteer at the center!

The manager of Pet-Palooza leads you down the hall to find Amber, the head volunteer. She's in a sunny room surrounded by dogs of different shapes and sizes. Amber introduces you to the pups, who bound over all at once, leaping and yipping excitedly.

Isabel pets a little Yorkie named Sugar. You're drawn to Pepper, a husky pup with sky-blue eyes. He seems to have more energy than all the other dogs put together.

As you walk around the room, Pepper chases after you. You toss a toy in the air, and he catches it. This is so fun! You turn to Amber and ask, "After you show us around, can I take Pepper outside to the play area?"

"Sure," Amber answers, "but keep an extra-close eye on Pepper. He sometimes runs away."

You can't imagine that. The husky pup is sticking pretty close to you. Your loyal pal is following you everywhere.

 Turn to page 10.

Sure enough, though, when you're working at Pet-Palooza a few days later, you hear a scritch-scratching and a high-pitched whine at the front door.

You glance up and see Pepper staring at you through the glass. He's not supposed to be at the center today—Thursday—but here he is, his leash dragging behind him and his owner nowhere in sight. Pet-Palooza is in a busy corner of the Shopping Square. You're horrified to think that Pepper was running around out there all by himself.

You open the door, and Pepper jumps all over you, covering you with sloppy dog kisses. It's like he ran all this way just to pay you a visit. You lead him into Pet-Palooza so that you can ask the manager what to do. She's out running an errand, but you find Amber in the back room.

Amber pours Pepper a bowl of water to help settle him down. Ten minutes later, a tall woman with her hair in a ponytail bursts through the door. It's Pepper's owner, Mrs. Thompson.

"Oh! I'm so glad he's here!" Mrs. Thompson exclaims.

"He's safe," Amber assures her, but you say nothing. You're wondering what took Mrs. Thompson so long. If Pepper were *your* dog, you'd never let him get away.

After that, you decide to take extra-special care of Pepper. You spend lots of time playing with him. You even start to pretend that he's your own.

 Turn to page 12.

A couple of weeks go by, and you've nearly forgotten about the incident. Pet-Palooza is buzzing with talk of the upcoming Parents' Day, a chance to show pet "parents" some of the tricks their pets learned while at Pet-Palooza. There will also be a craft and bake sale to raise money for a local animal shelter that cares for homeless animals. You're on your way to Pet-Palooza, thinking about what crafts you could make for the fund-raiser, when you spot a major commotion on the sidewalk ahead.

Several bouquets of flowers have fallen off a flower cart, and one bouquet seems to be rolling down the sidewalk— no, *running* down the sidewalk—in the jaws of a gray and white pup.

A bunch of girls are chasing the dog, laughing and shrieking as they try to grab the bouquet. With a burst of speed, the animal tears ahead of them. The dog stops and turns its head for just a moment before disappearing around a corner. It's *Pepper.*

If you take a shortcut to try to catch Pepper, turn to page 14.

If you run to join the girls who are following Pepper, turn to page 15.

You and the other girls run toward the fountain in the plaza.

"Hey!" Logan calls. "Look at this." She points to a trail of wet paw prints. You all let out a whoop as you track the prints toward a bush. Just then, Pepper bounds out and shakes cold water all over you.

"Eek!" you squeal. You reach down to grab Pepper before he can tear off again. No need to worry—he's already leaping up onto your legs, incredibly happy to see you. His tail is wagging sixty miles an hour.

"Awww, he's so adorable . . . and *wet*," says Neely.

If you tell the girls that you'll take Pepper to Pet-Palooza, turn to page 19.

If you spend a little time celebrating with your friends at the plaza, turn to page 20.

You run through an alley to try to cut Pepper off at the pass. He's too fast. He's already racing toward Five-Points Plaza, his leash dragging along behind him.

Pepper stops for a drink at the fountain and then dives into the water for a swim—but not for long. When he leaps out, you're within reach of his leash. You grab it firmly. Pepper yaps out a *Happy to see you!* Then he shakes his body to dry off—spraying you with cool water.

"What am I going to do with you?" you ask Pepper. He answers with a couple of wet kisses.

It's Saturday, a day when Pepper isn't normally at Pet-Palooza. That means he must have run away from home again. The thought makes you angry at the Thompsons, but you can't focus on that now. You have to figure out what to do. You don't know where the Thompsons live, but you could take Pepper to Pet-Palooza.

You hesitate. Your clothes are wet, plus you're almost as close to your room at Brightstar House as you are to Pet-Palooza. Pepper is looking up at you with his bright blue, trusting eyes.

 If you take Pepper back to your room so that you can change, turn to page 16.

 If you lead Pepper straight to Pet-Palooza, turn to page 19.

As you get closer, you spot your friends Neely and Riley in the crowd of girls. You race to catch up with them. "Which way did Pepper go?" you gasp.

"Wait, you know that dog?" asks Neely. "I think he went that way." Neely points toward Pet-Palooza.

Of course, you think. You speed toward Pet-Palooza with Riley keeping easy pace beside you. Neely and the other girls follow close behind. As you burst through the doors of Pet-Palooza, you find Isabel and another volunteer stocking dog toys. You ask if they have seen Pepper. "Nope, not today," says Isabel.

You rush to the outside play area to see if he's there. No sign of Pepper—only the other pups, barking at you to play.

Isabel steps out onto the sidewalk. She looks worried now, too. "Want me to help look?" she asks. You nod, still too breathless from running to say much. Isabel grabs her backpack and joins you.

 Turn to page 17.

You decide it can't hurt to make a quick stop to change your clothes. As you walk with Pepper toward your room at Brightstar House, you're stewing. Your heart is still racing from chasing Pepper and from the fear of seeing him running through the crowded Shopping Square all by himself. He could've gotten lost. You can't believe that Mrs. Thompson wasn't keeping a closer eye on Pepper. If he were your dog, you would.

If only he were my dog, you think. *I would give him all the exercise he needs, and never, ever let him feel lonely.*

When you get to your room, Pepper makes himself at home on the rug in your walk-in closet. Clearly he's tired from all of his mad dashing about! You dry him off with a towel and then change out of your own wet clothes.

When you're done, you see that Pepper has fallen asleep, his head resting on his paws. He looks so peaceful that you can't bear to wake him up to take him back to Pet-Palooza. Or maybe you can't bring yourself to say good-bye to Pepper, not knowing if he'll be safe with the Thompsons.

You lie down beside him, wrap your arm around his warm body, and bury your face in his soft gray fur. You're tired from all that running, too, and you're so comfy, you could almost fall asleep.

 Turn to page 18.

The group of girls searching for Pepper has grown. Logan is there now, and she's trying to help everyone decide where to search next. She loves to solve mysteries and figure things out. If anyone can help, it's her.

"If you were a dog," Logan says, "where would *you* go?"

"Where there's water?" offers Riley, holding up her water bottle.

You think about Pepper's peppy personality. He likes to play and run. He loves people and lots of action. That's probably why he's drawn to Pet-Palooza and the busy Shopping Square.

"Pepper loves crowds and commotion," you tell your friends. "I know! Five-Points Plaza has a water fountain *and* lots of action."

Logan agrees. "I bet Pepper is swimming in the water fountain as we speak," she says.

"Surrounded by a lot of wet girls," you add. "Let's go!" You take off running again.

 Turn to page 13.

A knock on the door startles you. Should you answer it? Luckily, Pepper is still asleep, so you step out of the closet and shut the door partway. "Who is it?" you call.

It's Isabel. "I'm making puppy bandannas to sell at the fund-raiser," she says, holding one up. "These are the safe kind that come off easily and never have to be tied."

You nod. "Cute!" you say. "You're so good at sewing."

"Want to help?" asks Isabel. "It would be fun to work together."

"Sure would be," you say. You're on the verge of telling Isabel about Pepper. She'll understand why you brought Pepper to your room. You can't get the words out, though. You're not ready for Pepper to go back to the Thompsons just yet.

Isabel stares at you curiously, as if she can tell that something's wrong. She knows you all too well.

You look away. The fact is, it's hard to think about raising money for homeless dogs when you have a pup in your own room who needs a safer home. "Sorry, Isabel," you finally say. "I'm just too busy right now. Too much homework."

Isabel looks disappointed as she leaves your room. You feel bad about keeping such a big secret from her. You know you can't keep Pepper forever. You just need time to figure out what to do.

 Turn to page 22.

As you walk with Pepper toward Pet-Palooza, your anger starts to build. You can't believe the Thompsons let Pepper get away again—it's so unsafe. And why haven't they come looking for him?

When you walk in the door of Pet-Palooza, Amber does a double take. "Why is Pepper here with you?" she asks. "And how'd you get so wet?" She tosses you a towel and uses another to start drying Pepper.

You give Amber a super-quick version: "Pepper some-how got away from the Thompsons and was running through the Shopping Square. I caught up with him at the fountain in the plaza."

You pause and then say, "Um, how could the Thompsons let him . . ." You're trying to figure out a nice way to say what you're thinking, which is not so nice. What you really want to say is what terrible owners the Thompsons are.

 Turn to page 23.

"Wow," says Neely. "We could go into the dog-tracking business!"

"Pepper alone could keep us in business," you joke. "I wish we could keep him from running away again."

"If you were a dog," Neely asks Logan, "what would keep *you* from running away?"

"Logan wouldn't be a dog," says Riley. "She'd be a curious kitten."

But Logan has an answer: "Treats would keep me home," she says.

Riley has an answer, too: "Lots of exercise," she says.

"A sturdy leash," adds Isabel. "A super-stylish sturdy leash would keep me by your side."

Your friends are cracking you up, but they're also giving you some great ideas for how to get Pepper to stay—and to help out homeless pets through the Pet-Palooza fund-raiser.

If you bake puppy treats, turn to page 24.

If you raffle off dog-walking services, turn to page 28.

If you decorate leashes, turn to page 59.

You're at your desk finishing up your math homework when your closet door swings open and Pepper trots over, up from his nap. You bend down to pet him. He licks your face and then runs to the door.

It suddenly occurs to you that puppies need to go to the bathroom—often. What now? You need to take Pepper outside, but you're afraid someone will see you with him.

You glance at your watch. It's nearly noon, which is good. If you wait a few more minutes, most of your friends will be on their way to the Star Student Center for lunch.

When the coast seems clear, you hurry Pepper out of your room and down the hall. You make it out the back door of Brightstar House without passing anyone. Phew! Now you just have to figure out the safest place to let Pepper do his business before he has an accident.

If you head for the patch of trees behind Brightstar House, turn to page 25.

If you walk around Brightstar House toward the lakeshore, turn to page 26.

"Whoa, slow down," Amber says as she finishes drying off Pepper. "The Thompsons aren't bad owners. It's just that huskies love to run and chase things, and they're smart enough to find their way out of yards. They're expert escape artists."

"Wow, I didn't know that," you say. You give Pepper a scratch behind the ear. "It makes me even more worried for him, though. How can we keep him safe?"

"I think what Pepper needs is good obedience training," says Amber.

You nod. That sounds like a great idea. "Hey, can I help train him?" you ask.

"Maybe," says Amber, "if the Thompsons agree that he needs formal training." Then she winks and says, "We can definitely work on one command with Pepper starting right now."

"Which one?" you ask.

"*Stay*," says Amber, and you both start to giggle.

Pepper's ears perk up as if to say, *What? What's so funny?*

 Turn to page 64.

The day before the fund-raiser, you and Logan meet at Sweet Treats bakery. The bakery staff help you and Logan bake some amazing puppy treats—canine cookies made with safe ingredients that dogs love.

You make a few batches of treats for people, too, called "Pupcakes"—cupcakes decorated to look like puppy faces. Some look like Honey, with peanut butter cookies for ears. Others look like Coconut, with real coconut sprinkled over vanilla icing. You decorate Pupcakes with blue candies for eyes, like Pepper's!

You bake a batch of puppy treats to sell at the fund-raiser and another to take to the animal shelter in town. You let Pepper sample a canine cookie, which he loves. You're pretty sure these treats will come in handy the next time you want Pepper to "stay." Who wouldn't stay for such a sweet treat? *Woof!*

The End

You head into the trees behind Brightstar House. Pepper is so excited to be outside that he can hardly stand it. He runs around in circles, sniffing everything. You tug lightly on his leash to hurry him along. You can't be out here all day—you run the risk of being seen.

Finally, after what seems like ages, Pepper is done. He stares up at you as if to say, *Where are we going next?*

On the way back into Brightstar House, your stomach growls. You think about grabbing a sandwich, but then you realize that Pepper must be hungry, too. You have to feed him! After sneaking him back into your room, you grab your backpack and hurry to Pet-Palooza for dog food.

There's no sign of Amber at Pet-Palooza. The volunteer at the desk says that Amber is helping the Thompsons track down Pepper, who is on the loose again. Oh, boy. You feel a twinge of guilt, but you also feel relief. With Amber gone you won't have to explain why you're buying a bag of dog food. You quickly hand over your money, stuff the bulky bag inside your backpack, and hurry home.

Turn to page 30.

You walk through the trees alongside Brightstar House all the way to the lake beyond. The grass along the shoreline is tall, and Pepper romps around, sniffing the ground and chasing dragonflies. Every few seconds, he turns around and runs back to you. He licks or nuzzles your hand, and you feel your heart melt.

You let Pepper lead you all the way to the beach, where he trots down to the water, leaving paw prints in the sand.

When Pepper reaches the water, he takes a quick drink. Then he spots something on the beach beside him. Suddenly, he rolls over and starts rubbing his back in the sand, as if he has an itch.

You can't help laughing—until you get closer and see what he's rolling in. You smell the fish before you see it.

"Pepper—that's disgusting!" you say, giving his leash a quick tug to get him away from the dead fish. He gives it one more sniff before reluctantly walking away.

Turn to page 29.

Riley thinks that raffling off dog-walking services is a great idea. "I bet lots of girls would jump at the chance to help walk the dogs," she says.

You say good-bye to your friends and take Pepper to Pet-Palooza. Amber is thrilled that you found him. While she calls the Thompsons, you run your fund-raising idea by the manager of Pet-Palooza. She likes the idea, but only if all of the dog walkers take the pet-sitter course so that they can do the job safely.

Neely designs a sign for the Parents' Day raffle: a cute picture of girls walking dogs in the meadow. Lots of your friends sign up to be dog walkers, and the raffle is a success—you earn more than $250 to donate to the animal shelter in town!

To top it off, Mrs. Thompson stops by your booth with an exciting request. "You did such a great job of finding Pepper," she says. "Would you be willing to walk him on a regular basis?"

"Sure, I'd love that!" you tell her. You beam from ear to ear, because this means that you'll be seeing a lot of Pepper in the coming weeks.

 Turn to page 33.

When you get back to your room, you realize that the smell of fish is still with you. Pepper reeks of it. You don't have a tub to wash him in, so you scrub him gently with a wet, soapy washcloth. It helps a little, you think.

At dinnertime, you take Pepper out for a bathroom break—steering clear of the lake this time. Then you race over to the Student Center to grab a sandwich. You bring some chicken back for Pepper, who eagerly gobbles it up.

By bedtime, waves of the fishy smell are still wafting from Pepper. You do your best to keep him out of your bed. He sits on the floor beside you, whining.

"Pepper, you smell like a fish market," you tell him, and he whines again as if he understands that you disapprove of his "cologne." Finally, you decide that hearing him cry is worse than smelling him, so you let him come up, as long as he stays on top of the covers, down by your feet.

Pepper curls up happily and falls asleep, but you lie awake. It was a crazy day, and your mind is racing with worry about what you'll do with him tomorrow.

You dream that Pepper buries a pile of rotten fish in your closet. Your closet ends up stinking so badly that someone from the university comes to inspect it—and finds Pepper. You wake up in a cold sweat, with Pepper licking your face.

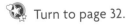 Turn to page 32.

When you open the door to your room, you're horrified. It looks as if it snowed paper inside—a real Arctic blizzard! There are torn scraps everywhere, but from what?

Then, your stomach sinking, you see Pepper lying in the middle of the floor, gnawing on a book. You gently pry it from his jaws and flip to the front cover. You gulp down a wave of dread. It's your math book, destroyed.

You start to scold Pepper, but then you realize it's
your fault. Pepper was only doing what pups do. In your
panic over buying dog food and getting out of Pet-Palooza
quickly, you forgot to buy an essential item: a chew toy.
This sure is getting complicated.

If you decide you can't leave Pepper alone anymore,
turn to page 34.

If you head back to Pet-Palooza for some chew toys,
turn to page 65.

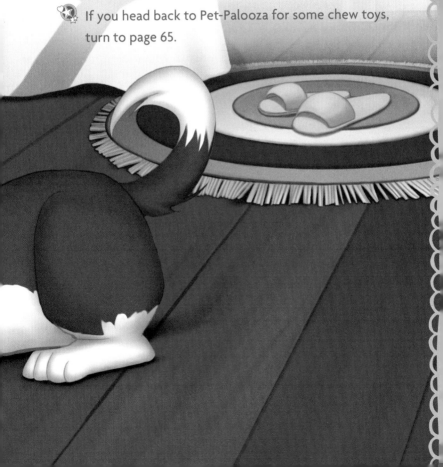

The next morning, you listen for the sound of other girls leaving their rooms. Then you sneak Pepper outside for a bathroom break. He still smells, but it's better today than it was yesterday. Or have you just gotten used to it?

After bringing Pepper back to your room, you dash to the Student Center, hoping to catch breakfast. You gulp down some cereal and juice. As you're returning your tray, Isabel waves to you from across the room.

"Did you hear about Pepper running away again?" she asks.

You nod distractedly.

"Do you want to help look for him this afternoon?" Isabel asks.

You feel your face flush with guilt. You feel awful, but you can't leave Pepper alone in your room for long, and there's no sense searching for a dog who's not exactly lost. "I wish I could help," you say, "but I don't have time."

Isabel's face falls. Just as you turn to walk away, Isabel wrinkles her nose and asks, "Ew, what's that smell? It's like rotten tuna or something."

Now you're beginning to sweat. "Um, I dunno," you mumble. "Maybe we're having fish for lunch?" Isabel looks doubtful, but you don't give her time to realize that the smell is coming from you. "Gotta go!" you exclaim as you hurry out of the cafeteria.

 Turn to page 35.

After the open house, Neely invites you all to her room to celebrate. Isabel gives each girl a bandanna she made, and Riley shows you how to do the "Downward Dog" yoga pose. Everyone gets a laugh out of that.

Neely hands you a drawing. "Specially made for you, as head of the raffle," she says. The girls circle around, murmuring their approval.

At the top of the picture, Neely wrote, "If you were a dog (or cat) . . ." Underneath, she painted your friends as animals. Isabel is a poodle with curly red hair and glasses. Neely is a white Westie wearing a beret and holding a paintbrush in her mouth. Riley is a golden retriever, and Logan is a curious brown kitten (of course!). Then there's you—a husky puppy who looks an awful lot like Pepper.

"I love it!" you gush, giving Neely a bear hug. You're grateful to her and to all of the girls. You did a good thing today, but you couldn't have done it without your best friends by your side.

The End

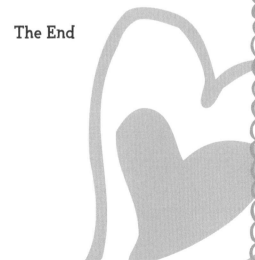

Pepper looks up at you and whines. "I don't blame you, boy," you say. "I left you all alone in a strange new place."

Pepper plunks his front paws on your knees and barks. Scratching his ears, you make him a promise: "I'll stay with you. I'll make sure you have fun stuff to play with, too."

You find a couple of tennis balls in your gym bag and toss them for Pepper to chase. He loves this, but after a few tosses, he sits down and whines, reminding you that he must be hungry and thirsty.

You pour water into a bowl. Pepper eagerly laps it up. Next, you give him some doggie nuggets and sit beside him while he crunches on his food. Caring for a puppy sure is a lot of work! You can manage it on a weekend, but what about when you're in class next week?

After Pepper eats, you play more, even though you're tired and hungry. In fact, your stomach's been tied up with knots of worry and hunger since lunchtime. Luckily, there's a granola bar in your backpack. It'll have to do.

 Turn to page 38.

When you get back to your room, the fishy smell greets you at the door. So does Pepper, with a chew toy in his mouth—only it's *not* a chew toy. It's one of your new tennis shoes, with a gaping hole in the toe. Ack!

You quickly slide out of the shoes you're wearing and put them on your bookshelf for safekeeping. Then you take a step into the room. Your foot instantly lands in something wet. Apparently Pepper needed another bathroom break.

"Oh, Pepper," you say, sinking down beside him. "What am I going to do with you?"

Pepper looks up at you and whines. He's waiting for you to do something, but you don't know what to do. He obviously needs to run off some of that energy. Amber told you that huskies need oodles of exercise. But you can't exactly take Pepper for a jog on campus when there are lost-dog signs plastered everywhere. So how can you look after him any better than the Thompsons did?

Pepper trusted you to take care of him, but you've done a horrible job. Taking care of a puppy is a lot more work than you thought it was, and you're pretty sure you can't do it anymore.

 If you take Pepper to Pet-Palooza, turn to page 39.

 If you leave Pepper in your room and go looking for Amber, turn to page 41.

You close the gate behind you to make sure none of the other pups get out of the play area. In the time it took you to latch the gate, you lost sight of Pepper. Running through town looking for him, you understand for the first time what the Thompsons have been going through. You didn't do anything wrong. You just couldn't control Pepper.

Isabel catches up to you. "There he goes!" she hollers, pointing toward Cute Collectibles. The door to the gift shop is ajar, and you run in together and start searching the aisles for Pepper. You hear him before you see him. He's barking at a woman's oversize purse. Why on earth would he bark at a purse? It's not until you get closer that you see the woman has a tiny Chihuahua tucked into it!

You take a firm hold of Pepper's leash. He follows you out of the shop, his head low and his tail between his legs. You want to pet him to reassure him that you're not mad, but you remember what Amber said about consistency. You lead Pepper to the sidewalk, where you ask him to sit and stay. He does, perfectly. You can tell that he wants to please you to make up for running away.

"Very nice," says Amber, who just ran over from Pet-Palooza. "I think you've got the hang of this—both of you!"

All the way back to Pet-Palooza, Pepper stays close by your side. He may not always do everything you ask him to do, but he *is* a sweet, loyal dog.

 Turn to page 72.

Sunday morning, someone knocks on your door. You poke your head into the hallway. "Hey, what's going on?" you ask Isabel.

Isabel looks shocked to see that you're still in your pajamas. "There's a meeting at Pet-Palooza to talk about Parents' Day," she says. "Don't you remember?"

Your face falls. "Oh, right," you say. "Sorry, I'm still swamped with work."

Isabel arches her eyebrow and then walks away. She's clearly hurt, but you have to focus on what's best for Pepper, and that means not leaving him alone.

You spend the day playing and snuggling with the pup. While he naps, you do manage to grab food at the Student Center, because you're seriously starving. But you hurry right back.

Already, you can't imagine life without Pepper. But tomorrow is Monday, and you need to attend classes. You'll have to figure out what to do with Pepper—fast.

 Turn to page 44.

Pepper seems happy to be back on the leash, heading toward Pet-Palooza. He's also clearly happy to be getting some exercise. You don't pass anyone you know on the way, and you're grateful for that. You wonder how many of your friends are out searching for Pepper right now.

As you round the corner toward Pet-Palooza, you spot Amber taping a poster to a streetlamp. She looks up at you, waves, and then glances up again—shocked to see Pepper standing beside you.

"You found Pepper! Where was he?" Amber exclaims, dropping the stack of posters and rushing to your side. She gives Pepper a huge hug. Then, before you have time to answer her, Amber pulls away from the pup with a disgusted look on her face. "Yuck, Pepper," she says. "You got into something gross, didn't you? Let's get you cleaned up and call your family."

Amber takes Pepper by the leash and hurries into Pet-Palooza to call the Thompsons. You follow, trying to think of what to say. Amber is so excited about Pepper's return that you can't imagine how you'll tell her the truth about what happened.

 If you let Amber believe that you found Pepper, turn to page 46.

 If you tell Amber that you've been hiding Pepper, turn to page 48.

Pepper's howling stops the second you open the closet door. "I have some treats for you," you say, bending to pet him. Pepper is so excited to see you that his whole body wags from side to side. You pretend not to see the chewed-up sock at your feet, and you vow never to leave Pepper alone again—at least not again today.

You're playing with Pepper when a knock on your door startles you. You put Pepper back in your closet with a chew toy, and then you open your door. It's Neely.

"Did you hear that Pepper ran away again?" Neely asks. "I'm making posters, and I need a description of Pepper's personality. Isabel said you know him well. What can you tell me?" Neely holds a notebook, her pen poised to write.

This is *so* not the right time for this, but talking about Pepper is easy. "He's a ball of energy," you say, "and he loves to be in the middle of any activity. He likes to chew things." You giggle nervously at that. "He loves to play, and—"

In the middle of your sentence, you hear a scratching at the closet door behind you. Pepper is bored with his new chew toy already? No, he just wants to be the center of attention, as you explained to Neely a moment ago.

"What was that?" Neely asks, trying to see around you.

 If you tell Neely the truth, turn to page 43.

 If you make something up, turn to page 58.

You leave Pepper in the closet again, putting anything he can chew on out of reach. You hurry toward Pet-Palooza, where you find Amber taping posters on streetlamps. She can tell that you're upset, which makes it easier to confess to her what you've done—and why. "I wanted to protect Pepper from getting lost or hurt . . ." you say, your eyes brimming with tears.

Amber takes it all in. She says that she needs to call the Thompsons right away—and tell the manager that Pepper has been found. Afterward, Amber walks you back to your room. While you walk, she says, "Dogs like Pepper need tons of care. They also need a lot of training."

"I totally get that now," you assure her.

"Good," Amber replies. "By the way, the Thompsons asked me on the phone if we could help them train Pepper so that he stays at home and doesn't run away."

"That's great," you say. You're relieved to know that something good will come of this, but you're dreading the moment when you'll have to say good-bye to Pepper— especially when Amber says that you may need to take a couple of weeks off from Pet-Palooza. She doesn't call it punishment, but you're pretty sure it is.

"After that," Amber says, "you can come back and see Pepper. And just maybe," she adds with a smile, "you can help me train that pup to *stay*."

The End

On Monday, you and Amber take Pepper out into the play area to start training. Amber shows you the sit command first. "A dog needs to know how to sit before he can *stay* sitting," she says. "Make sense?"

Amber teaches you to say "sit" in a firm voice while pulling up on Pepper's leash and gently pushing down on his back. Pepper seems to already know this command, because he performs it super fast. "Good job!" you tell him.

Amber says to keep practicing with Pepper for a while to reinforce the command. But after she goes back inside, Pepper doesn't seem interested in tricks anymore. He keeps bringing a ball over for you to toss to him.

You understand how Pepper feels. You're a little bored now, too, and you're worried that if you keep making him do something he doesn't want to do, he won't enjoy his time with you. Maybe that's what happened at the Thompsons'. Did they not play with him enough?

 If you give in and let Pepper play, turn to page 47.

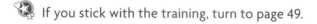 If you stick with the training, turn to page 49.

Neely is way too smart not to guess that something's up. Plus, she's a pretty good friend. It would be a major relief to tell someone what's going on. So you grit your teeth and ask, "Can you keep a secret?" Neely hesitates for a moment and then says yes. You invite her into your room and open the closet. Neely's jaw drops.

"But everyone's looking for Pepper!" she blurts out. "I'm supposed to make posters!"

You offer Neely a seat on your bed. "Pepper's owners take terrible care of him," you explain with a tremor in your voice. "I found him running loose in the Shopping Square, so I'm keeping him for his own good—to protect him." Pepper pads over and looks at you, and then Neely, with anxious eyes.

Neely's face has grown pale. "If what you say is true, something has to be done about it," she says. "But you can't keep Pepper forever. You know that, right?"

You sigh. "Yes, but I haven't quite decided what's the best thing to do for Pepper," you say. "I need a little more time. Will you keep my secret another day or two?"

Neely looks reluctant, but she smiles weakly and says, "For now."

 Turn to page 54.

You set your alarm clock for dawn on Monday to let Pepper out before the other girls wake up. You set down food and water in your closet. Then you reluctantly head out.

In the entryway to the Student Center, there's a "lost dog" poster with Pepper's picture on it. You stare at your feet and hurry past it. You gobble down breakfast and head to class. Afterward, you race to Pet-Palooza. You and Isabel are scheduled for a short shift. You just hope Pepper will be okay in your room till you get back.

Isabel is excited because she's going to watch Amber do some pet grooming today. Amber finishes bathing a terrier pup, and then she shampoos Sugar. Amber blow-dries Sugar's hair and gathers a lock of it into a tiny bow.

"Speaking of grooming," Isabel says, "you're shedding." You look down and see gray and white fur on your shirt.

You think fast. "Must be from petting Praline," you say. Praline the kitty has gray fur, too, but you'd recognize the fur on your shirt anywhere. It's Pepper's.

"I didn't see you playing with her today," says Isabel. Something about her tone of voice makes you nervous.

 If you head out to the puppy play area, turn to page 60.

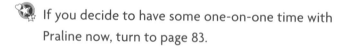 If you decide to have some one-on-one time with Praline now, turn to page 83.

Ribbons

Brushes

Toys

Treats

"But where did you find him?" Amber persists as you help her give Pepper a warm bath with anti-odor shampoo.

You don't want to lie, so you tell Amber *where* but not *when* you found Pepper. "I spotted him in the Shopping Square," you say. After all, you did find Pepper there. You just took your time bringing him back.

"At least he's safe now," says Amber. "Thanks to you."

More like safe from *me,* you think sadly. *Safe from getting into my things and from being holed up in my tiny room.*

"Do you want to wait for the Thompsons?" Amber asks you. "I'm sure they'll want to thank you."

You have mixed feelings about that. Now that you're feeling so connected to Pepper, you're afraid you'll feel a little jealous seeing him with the Thompsons. But you also feel guilty for keeping him in your room while they were searching for him. You decide that you don't want to be there when the Thompsons come for Pepper. You don't think you can bear it. You give Pepper a quick hug good-bye and hurry toward the door.

 Turn to page 50.

Amber comes back outside and sees you and Pepper playing a game of catch. "You quit training already?" she asks. "If you want Pepper to be obedient and loyal to you, you have to stick with the training and follow through."

Amber promises that obedience training won't make Pepper like you any less, and says that he'll probably respect you even *more*.

That all makes sense. Amber is pretty smart about these things. You decide to give training another go the next time you come in.

 Turn to page 49.

If you want him to be loyal to you, you have to follow through.

INNERSTAR UNIVERSITY

After Amber hangs up the phone, you take a deep breath, and then you tell her the truth about finding Pepper yesterday and hiding him in your room. Amber looks shocked for the second time today. She says nothing.

"I was only trying to protect him," you continue, "to be a loyal friend to him. I'm worried that Pepper will keep running away from the Thompsons. What if next time, he gets completely lost—or even hurt?"

After a long pause, Amber gives you a sad smile. "Let's talk more about it later," she says, taking Pepper's leash. "I need to get him cleaned up and ready for the Thompsons, who will be here any minute."

When Mrs. Thompson comes rushing through the door, Pepper runs to her and licks her face up and down, which breaks your heart. Maybe you were wrong about the Thompsons being bad owners. Maybe you were wrong about everything.

 If you wait to talk with Amber, turn to page 52.

 If you take the opportunity to slip out the door, turn to page 50.

On Wednesday, you take Pepper back into the yard, armed with doggie treats. You leash him and repeat the sit command about twenty-five times in a row, keeping it up even after Pepper starts acting distracted and bored.

Pepper seems to respect your firm voice, which reminds you of what Amber said about respect. You make sure to reward Pepper with treats and lots of praise.

When you show Amber how well Pepper is listening, you feel proud, and you think that Pepper is proud of himself, too. You can sort of tell by how he holds his body upright and perky, even though he's done the sit command so many times.

"I'm really impressed," says Amber, which means a lot to you. "Good work, Pepper!" she says, leaning over to pet him. "I think you're both ready to start working on the stay command now."

"Yaaay!" you shout as you skip around the yard. Pepper frolics at your heels. Training a puppy is a lot of work, but it's great fun to see the results.

 Turn to page 51.

You duck out the front door of Pet-Palooza. Girls say hello to you on the path back to Brightstar House, but you feel so sad and guilty that you just want to hide. You don't think you'll be able to go back to Pet-Palooza for a good long while. It'll hurt too much to see Pepper there.

As you hurry home, you feel like a runaway dog, keeping your head low and trying not to be spotted. You can't wait to get home so that you can crawl into bed and pull the covers over your head. When you finally do that, you feel a moment of relief—until the fish smell hits you.

You laugh bitterly, thinking of a twist on a classic saying: *You made your smelly old bed. Now you've got to hold your nose and lie in it.*

The End

On your next shift, Amber shows you the stay command. First you have Pepper sit, and then you say, "Stay." You're supposed to make him sit there until you pet under his chin or call for him, which tells him it's okay to move.

Amber explains that once Pepper aces that command, you should try it again while acting distracted. You should look around the yard or up at the sky—anywhere but at Pepper. The last step is to say the command and then walk a few feet away from Pepper to see if he stays.

This part turns out to be much harder than the sit command! Pepper will stay if you're standing right in front of him, but as soon as you step away, he leaps up after you. You try again and again, but you're incredibly frustrated.

"Pepper," you groan, "if you refuse to listen, then we won't get any playtime before my shift is over. Don't you want some playtime?" Pepper cocks his head at you and wags his tail.

 If you decide that obedience training isn't your thing, turn to page 53.

 If you ask Amber for more help, turn to page 56.

Amber doesn't tell Mrs. Thompson what you did, and you're grateful for that. But you can see that you've put Amber in a tough spot. She's trying to put on a happy face, but there's disappointment in her eyes.

"I was worried that something awful had happened to Pepper," Mrs. Thompson says. "My husband and I were out searching most of the day yesterday. Chloe, too."

You wonder who Chloe is.

"Yes, um, we were searching all day, too," Amber says. You can hear the strain in her voice. She goes on to describe ways to keep huskies safe, such as obedience training and sturdy fences, since huskies are expert diggers.

As you listen to Amber talk, you realize that you made a huge assumption in thinking that the Thompsons were bad owners. And you didn't think about what you were putting Amber through.

Pepper isn't the only friend you were disloyal to today. You'll have a lot of making up to do. You may as well start now.

If you ask Amber if you can help her out more around the day-care center, turn to page 55.

If you focus on fund-raising to help Pet-Palooza reach its goal, turn to page 110.

If you write a friendship poem for Amber, turn to page 63.

"I don't think I'm cut out for obedience training," you confess to Amber when she comes back outside. "I don't think I'm strict enough, or patient enough, or—"

Amber chuckles. "It's okay," she says. "Training dogs is not for everyone. Besides, you're really good at playing with Pepper, and he needs plenty of playtime, too." That's obvious by the way that Pepper is streaking around you and Amber at warp speed while you're talking. Pepper never seems to get enough play or exercise time!

Amber says that she'll take over training Pepper. You're relieved about that, but you'd still like to do something to help with Pepper's training. Then you have a sudden brainstorm. You can make a new leash for Pepper!

You find a pretty purple leash at Pet-Palooza. Later, in art class, Neely helps you stamp pink hearts all the way down the leash on both sides. The finished craft gives you an idea for the Parents' Day fund-raiser. You'll decorate a bunch of dog leashes!

 Turn to page 59.

The next day, there's a meeting at Pet-Palooza to talk about the fund-raiser. Neely doesn't want to go without you. You hate to leave Pepper, but you figure you owe Neely one, so you walk together to Pet-Palooza.

Along the way, you pass a "lost dog" poster. Seeing Pepper's sweet face on that poster makes you feel guilty, but you still think you're doing the right thing by keeping him.

At the meeting, Isabel shares her idea of making doggy bandannas to sell. Neely has an idea, too: she can sketch portraits of the pets and sell them to their owners.

"That would be great!" says Isabel. "You did a really good job drawing Pepper for those posters."

Neely mumbles a thank-you and stares at her hands. There's an awkward pause.

You break the silence by saying, "I wish the Thompsons would take better care of Pepper. How could they let him run away so many times?"

Isabel looks surprised. "You shouldn't judge the Thompsons so quickly," she says. "They're really nice, and they love Pepper a lot."

Neely glances at you with confusion and concern in her eyes. You look away.

 Turn to page 68.

Amber says that she'll ask the manager if there are ways you can help out more around Pet-Palooza. Later in the week, Amber calls you and says that there *is* something you can do: clean the animal cages. You hesitate for just a second before agreeing to help.

Cleaning cages isn't your favorite task, but you're happy to be doing something to make up for the mistakes you've made. Amber cleans alongside you, silently at first. Then she says, "I've spoken with the Thompsons about giving Pepper some obedience training. They're all for it."

"Good!" you say. "I'm relieved to hear that." But inside, you also feel guilty. You should've known from the start that Amber would know how to handle things.

You sigh and try to shake off the guilt. What counts now is that Amber has given you another chance. That's a gift, and you're determined not to take it for granted.

The End

Amber shows you how to bring the leash back into the training to help get Pepper to stay. Sure enough, the leash helps. If Pepper gets up or takes a step toward you, you gently pull up on his leash until he sits again.

After a while, Pepper gets pretty good at sitting and staying for you while you're alone with him in the play yard. You're finally ready for the true test: trying the command while the other pups are in the yard, too.

You lead Pepper out to the puppy play area. He sits and stays for you, even though Coconut is barking for him to play. *Pretty impressive*, you think. But Pepper is sniffing at the air—he's caught a scent. Or is it that he caught sight of Isabel coming in the back gate?

Suddenly, Pepper is off like a shot. One minute the leash is in your hand, and the next, it's trailing behind Pepper. He bolts through the open gate and tears off across the meadow.

Oh, no, here we go again, you think as you take off after him.

If you fly out of the play area after Pepper, go online to innerstarU.com/secret and enter this code: LOYAL4EVER

If you stop to close the gate safely behind you, turn to page 37.

"What's that scratching sound?" Neely asks again.

"Probably mice," you say, shrugging your shoulders.

"You're kidding!" Neely says, taking a step backward.

"No, I'm not. A few critters are camped out in the walls," you say matter-of-factly. "Don't you have mice?"

"Ewww! You're freaking me out," Neely cries as she races out of your room.

You giggle and close the door. That was pretty funny, but it could have easily gone wrong—like if Pepper had started barking. And now that Neely's gone, you're still faced with the challenge of taking care of Pepper, which is pretty overwhelming.

You make it through the weekend without any more visits from friends—or mice. You sneak Pepper out when the other girls are at meals or sleeping, which means keeping weird hours. You're tired, and you have a stomach-ache from eating too many meals on the run. You love hanging out with Pepper, but you're worried about what you'll do when Monday comes and you have to head back to class.

 Turn to page 44.

You have a sleepover and invite your friends to help you decorate leashes for Parents' Day. Pet-Palooza donated a whole box of leashes in bright colors, just waiting for some handiwork.

Logan stamps paw prints on her leashes. Neely draws little dog bones. Isabel stamps pink, blue, and purple stars on her leashes.

You stick with hearts. The heart-stamped leashes are a reminder of how much love you feel for Pepper, and for all the pets who will wear the leashes and be safer because of them.

On Parents' Day, your friends help you run your craft booth. The leashes sell like hotcakes, and you make a lot of money to help the local shelter.

You are proud that you found a way to help keep dogs safe. You're grateful to your friends, too, who "stayed" by your side to help make the fund-raiser a success!

The End

Isabel follows you. You sit side by side, watching the pups playing. Coconut scampers away, and Honey wiggles her rear end in the air, preparing for the chase.

"You don't seem all that worried about Pepper," Isabel finally says. "Do you know where he is?"

You can't look at her. You don't want to lie to Isabel. She knows you better than most girls do. She knows how much you love Pepper, too. She knows your secret—she must.

"Pepper is safe," you say in a small voice. "He's with me."

Isabel nods. She doesn't seem surprised.

"Are you going to tell Amber?" you ask.

"I was hoping *you* would," Isabel says gently.

But you can't—not yet. You shake your head.

Isabel is silent for a moment. "You can't keep him," she says. "You'll get caught and get in trouble with Amber. And I don't want to work here without you."

You're surprised to see how sad Isabel looks. But you still don't know if she's going to tell Amber about Pepper. That upsets you. Isabel is *your* friend. She should keep your secret no matter what, shouldn't she?

 Turn to page 62.

You and Isabel sit together in painful silence. It's a relief when Amber calls you in to watch her and the Pet-Palooza manager give Sugar a "pet-icure," or a nail clipping. Sugar doesn't seem to like the procedure much. She squirms and tries to escape Amber's arms.

"Does it hurt her?" you ask, leaning in closer.

"No," says the manager. "If we do it right and clip only the tips, Sugar shouldn't feel it at all. She's just a little nervous, and she hates to keep still."

"Don't we know it!" says Isabel. You all laugh a little, which breaks some of the tension.

"If we do this for Sugar often enough," says Amber, "she'll learn to trust us. She'll realize that we're just doing what's best for her."

At those words, Isabel looks up at you. You quickly look away. You can hardly wait for your shift to end so that you can get back to Pepper.

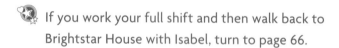 If you work your full shift and then walk back to Brightstar House with Isabel, turn to page 66.

 If you ask Amber if you can leave early, turn to page 86.

You go out in the play yard and spend time with the pups. Soon, you're inspired to get out your notebook and write Amber a poem. You know you broke her trust, and you'd like to earn it back. You write a few lines:

> Your friendship means a lot to me,
> and you've been loyal and true.
> That's why I will work so hard
> to make things up to you.

You close your notebook thoughtfully. You don't know if your words will make a difference, but they're a good start.

The End

Amber calls the Thompsons to let them know that Pepper is safe. It turns out that he got loose chasing another dog at the market near the Shopping Square, and the Thompsons are definitely eager for Pepper to learn obedience training. Amber gives you a thumbs-up even before she's off the phone.

Amber takes Pepper outside to play until his owners come to get him. You follow her out. "So, let's start training Pepper on your next shift," she suggests.

"I'd love that!" you say.

"Right now, though," Amber says, pointing to your wet outfit, "go home and get dry."

You shiver, suddenly remembering how wet—and cold—you are. You head for home, but you can hardly wait until Monday, your next shift at Pet-Palooza. Training Pepper will be fun—and pretty easy, too, if Pepper is as smart as Amber says he is. Who knows? Pepper may even ace the commands after his first few tries, which would leave you plenty of time to play with him.

 Turn to page 42.

Before heading back to Pet-Palooza, you put Pepper in your walk-in closet, along with a bowl full of water. Your closet is a big, safe space, and it'll keep Pepper from chewing up anything in your bedroom.

At Pet-Palooza, you buy three kinds of toys: a rubber bone, a chew ball, and a ball on a rope. You can't wait to give them to Pepper!

When you get back to Brightstar House, you hurry down the hall. You pass Neely's room, where you can hear her practicing the saxophone. Then, above the saxophone, you hear something else: a dog howling.

Neely's playing stops abruptly, but the howling doesn't. Neely pokes her head out the door. "What's that noise?" she asks you, her freckled face puckered up with confusion.

"I dunno," you say quickly. "A siren?"

Neely pauses with her mouth open, as if she's about to state a different theory. You don't want to hear it, because it may well be the right one. You hug your Pet-Palooza bag to your chest and hurry to your room.

Turn to page 40.

On the walk home, Isabel starts chatting about Parents' Day. "I'm going to sell the bandannas, but I'm also making a few extras so that the pups at the center can model them," she says excitedly.

"That's a cute idea," you say. You picture the dogs walking like models down a runway.

Isabel counts them off on her fingers. "I'll make a pink one for Coconut, a green one for Honey, and a blue one for Pepper. Won't blue look great with Pepper's eyes?" she asks.

You can't believe Isabel is bringing up Pepper. As you walk, though, you keep picturing Pepper wearing that blue bandanna. You wish that none of this had happened—that you could go back to last week, when you and Isabel were happily planning for the fund-raiser.

You give Isabel a quick good-bye at her door and hurry on to your own room. When you open your door, you can't believe your eyes.

Now your room looks like a blizzard in progress! Feathers are floating through the air, caught on the breeze of your open window. Some are wafting down onto your rug, turning it white. Your bedspread looks like a down quilt turned inside out. Even Pepper is covered. He looks like a snowbird, trying to shake off his feathers. The whole scene would be funny if it weren't so incredibly awful.

Pepper must have torn apart a pillow—no, two! You race around, picking up what's left of them.

"Oh, Pepper," you wail, as he slinks toward the closet. "What am I going to do with you?"

"What did he do?" someone calls from your doorway. Your pulse skips a few beats as you wheel around. You forgot to close the door all the way, and Isabel is peeking in. She looks around your room, puts a hand to her mouth, and gasps. "Yipes," she says. "What *are* you going to do?"

If you decide it's time to give Pepper back, turn to page 74.

If you say to Isabel, "Nothing—Pepper and I are just fine," turn to page 70.

On the way home from Pet-Palooza, Neely is quiet. She kicks a pebble along the path ahead of her. "Maybe it's time for you to turn Pepper in," she says finally. "What Isabel said kind of got to me, you know?" She glances at you for your reaction.

You're upset that Isabel convinced Neely so easily. Neely is supposed to be on your side. "Just because the Thompsons love Pepper doesn't mean that they are good dog owners," you say.

Neely falls silent again. You leave her at the door to her room and walk on toward yours without saying a word.

When you open the door to your room, out bounds Pepper. You have no idea how he got out of the closet, but now he's sprinting down the hall toward Neely.

"Catch him!" you holler. Neely lunges, but Pepper's way too fast. The two of you chase him down the long hallway, down the staircase, and right out the side door, which someone left propped open.

 Turn to page 94.

Isabel shakes her head and walks away as you close your door behind her.

You sink down on your rug in a pile of feathers. The truth is, you don't have a clue what you're going to do. You're in way over your head.

Pepper comes out of the closet, shakes off again, and settles next to you, licking your face. You love him so much, but is loving him enough? You tried to keep Pepper safe, but you don't have the time or the space to give him what he really needs.

You have a good cry and then slowly start picking up your room. You're getting ready to vacuum when you hear your door open. It's Isabel again. Her face is pale.

"I'm sorry," she says, "but I couldn't keep your secret anymore." Isabel steps into the room, and you see, with horror and humiliation, that Amber is standing behind her.

Amber looks angry, but all she says is, "I need to take Pepper back now. Do you have his leash?" You hand it over to her. What else can you do?

You can't cry—you're all cried out. You can't protect Pepper anymore. You wonder if you ever really could. And you probably can't work at Pet-Palooza anymore, either— not after what you've done.

It takes you almost two hours to pick up all the white feathers in your room. You've already spent your piggy-bank money on a replacement math book, so you can't buy new pillows. You'll have to make do for a while with your rolled-up T-shirts.

Isabel and you are on the outs for now, too. You're starting to realize, though, that this entire mess with Pepper was your fault, not Isabel's. She was only trying to be a good friend to you, just as you tried to be to Pepper. All you can do now is try to figure out how things got so mixed up—and how you can set them right again.

The End

You continue training Pepper, and you can hardly wait for Parents' Day so that you can show the Thompsons what he can do. Finally, it's the big day! Amber and Isabel lead the dogs out wearing their colorful bandannas. The owners clap and cheer, which sets off some of the dogs barking— a perfect time for the manager to introduce the obedience part of the event. This is it!

As you lead Pepper in front of the audience, you wonder if he'll be able to obey commands before such a big crowd. Over the weeks, you've worked with Pepper around all the other puppies, so he's had lots of practice ignoring distractions. But this is different—this is a people crowd.

You talk to Pepper in a soothing voice. "Sit," you say. You try to get him to focus solely on you. It's working. He's looking right at you, waiting for your next command.

When you're pretty sure Pepper is calm and focused, you say, in a firm voice, "Stay." Then you take a few steps away, while continuing to face him.

Finally, you turn your back and walk away from him— all the way to the other side of the play area. This is the real test. Your heart is pounding. Can he handle it? When you turn around, he's still sitting, watching you expectantly.

"Come, Pepper!" you say. At this, he sprints to you, his tail wagging wildly. The crowd applauds, and you nearly burst with pride.

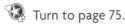 Turn to page 75.

You raise your hands in the air. "What *can* I do?" you exclaim as you look mournfully at Isabel. "Pepper is ruining my room because he's not getting enough exercise. I can't keep him—you were right about that."

Isabel looks as if she doesn't want to be right. "I'll go with you to Pet-Palooza," she offers.

You sigh. "Thanks," you say. "I'm not sure I can face Amber—or say good-bye to Pepper—all on my own."

Isabel holds Pepper's leash while you shuffle the worst of the pillow mess to a corner. Then she walks with you to Pet-Palooza. As you walk, you reach out for Isabel's hand. Funny how you could be upset with her one moment, yet so grateful for her the next.

You're relieved to find that Amber is the only person working the desk at Pet-Palooza. You sure don't want an audience for this. Amber listens to your story, while Isabel stands by your side.

"I'm disappointed in you," Amber admits. "But I'm really glad you made the decision to bring Pepper back."

 Turn to page 80.

After the show, Mrs. Thompson, a tall lady in a V-neck sweater, approaches you. She shakes your hand, as if you were a grown-up. "I want to compliment you on your work with Pepper," she says. "You really know how to get him to listen."

"Thanks," you say. "Pepper's full of energy, that's for sure. But it's not that hard to train him, once he gets the hang of it—and knows who is boss."

Mrs. Thompson introduces you to her daughter, Chloe, who looks just a little younger than you. Chloe has her mom's wavy hair and welcoming eyes.

"Could you teach Chloe how to do the 'sit and stay' command with Pepper?" asks Mrs. Thompson.

You're not sure you'd know how. Training a pup is one thing. Training a *person* to train a pup is different.

Chloe chimes in, "I think it would help me a lot when I'm playing with Pepper in the park near my house." She grins sheepishly, as if she was the one who lost control of Pepper the last time he got away.

 If you agree to try to teach Chloe, turn to page 79.

 If you tell Mrs. Thompson that Amber would be the better teacher, turn to page 81.

It takes you a while to think up a fund-raising idea. It finally comes to you while you're looking at the Web site for the animal shelter.

The shelter posts pictures of all the animals you can sponsor. When you *sponsor* a pet, you don't bring it home, but you offer a little money to help that pet stay safely in the shelter until someone else can adopt him or her. You think sponsoring a pet is a little bit like how you can care for Pepper. He'll never be *your* pup, but you love him and want to help keep him safe.

You print out pictures of some of the animals and use them to decorate a booth at Parents' Day. Then you make a sign asking people to sponsor the pets by donating money. Lots of people do! By the end of the event, you've helped to sponsor twelve pets. You feel good knowing that your love for Pepper will help other animals in need.

Neely's art booth is a success, too. After the open house, Neely brings you a picture she painted. It's of Pepper running along the lakeshore, chasing a butterfly. You *love* the picture. Pepper may not be your pup, but he'll always be your good and loyal friend—just like Neely.

The End

You run to Pet-Palooza, hoping that Pepper found his way back there. Sure enough, when you burst through the doors of the center, there's Pepper, sitting on the floor beside Amber. You gasp.

"Isn't it great?" says Amber. "Neely found him!"

Neely? You have to close your gaping mouth and force a smile onto your face. "That's, um, g-good news," you stammer. "Where did she find him?"

Amber frowns. "I don't know," she says. "Neely just said that she found Pepper somewhere near Brightstar House."

You breathe a sigh of relief. At least Neely kept that part of the story to herself. Still, you're pretty sure she took Pepper from your room, and you can't believe she betrayed you that way. You thought she was your friend.

It looks as if Pepper is your only true friend, and you're losing him now, too. As you turn and leave Pet-Palooza, your heart feels so heavy you can barely breathe.

 Turn to page 99.

Chloe brings Pepper to Pet-Palooza one afternoon so that you can show her the sit and stay commands. You start with the sit command using the leash.

At first, Pepper looks to you, confused about why Chloe is training him. It's amazing to think about how loyal he is to you now. All of your time and training with him have really paid off. Dog training is a little like friendship: the more you put into it, the more you get out of it.

"Sit," Chloe commands Pepper. After a few times, Pepper starts to listen to the prompts of his new trainer. You give Chloe a high five, and you realize that you're just as excited for her as you were when Pepper first obeyed you! Pepper can be loyal to you *and* to Chloe.

You check your watch and see that your shift is almost up. "Next time, I'll help you work on the stay command," you promise Chloe.

"Thanks," she says. "When I'm better at giving Pepper commands, maybe you could come to our park and play Frisbee with us?"

"I'd love that!" you say. As you watch Chloe lead Pepper away, you smile. Who would have thought that Pepper's great escape might lead to something so wonderful—a whole new friendship!

The End

Saying good-bye to Pepper is the hardest part of all, but as you gaze into his friendly eyes and kiss his soft forehead, you picture him wearing that blue bandanna and strutting his stuff on Parents' Day. You're glad you brought him back when you did so that he can take part in the fund-raiser. If you set things right with Amber, maybe you can be there, too.

It takes a few minutes to muster up the courage, but on your way out the door, you ask Amber if you can still help with the fund-raiser.

If you ask Amber if you can help Isabel with the bandannas, turn to page 88.

If you ask Amber what part of the fund-raiser she needs the most help with, turn to page 85.

"Amber's the real pro," you tell the Thompsons. "She's probably the best one to ask."

"Of course," says Mrs. Thompson. "We'll ask Amber."

As the Thompsons walk away, you feel a twinge of regret that you aren't going to teach Chloe what you know. It's not much, but it's enough to help with Pepper's "running away" problem, and no one needs those tips more than Pepper's own family.

You're surprised the next day when you go to Pet-Palooza for your shift and find Chloe waiting by the front entrance. "Hi," she says shyly. "Amber convinced me to sign up for the pet-sitting course."

"That's great!" you tell her. "I'll show you where the course meets." You lead Chloe into Pet-Palooza's classroom, grateful for the chance to help her.

You hope that if Chloe comes to Pet-Palooza on a regular basis, you'll get to know her better. You may be able to spend more time with the pup you love. And who knows? You might make a new friend, too!

The End

You take Praline into the kitty cuddling area. Two white kittens are in there already, playing a game of hide-and-pounce. An orange tabby is grooming herself in the corner.

You don't really know cats—you're much more of a dog person. But Praline is so cute, and she thinks the feathery toy you're dangling is the next best thing to tuna fish.

She pounces on the toy, chases it, and rolls onto her back to bat at it. Then she suddenly leaps up and streaks around the room, only to dive-bomb the toy again. She has mega-watts of energy for being such a tiny thing.

You giggle as you watch Praline, but then you think of Pepper. You know that he needs tons of playtime and space, too. You feel bad that he doesn't have more room to play in your room.

It's no wonder Pepper is using his pent-up energy to chew things. You imagine what he might be doing right now, and the image of your math book chewed to pieces flashes through your mind. You feel a rush of panic and decide to ask Amber if you can go home early.

 Turn to page 86.

Neely helps you out of the water. She follows you as you lead Pepper back to Brightstar House, bending over to clutch his collar with one hand.

"I'll dry Pepper while you take a shower," Neely suggests in a mom sort of way. You can't protest—your teeth are chattering too hard.

Under the steamy water, you replay the whole mad dash into the lake and wonder how things got so crazy. You comb your hair, jump into fresh clothes, and hurry out to your room.

"How's Pepper?" you ask.

"Muddy, but better," says Neely. She did a good job of rubbing Pepper dry. He's snuggled beside her, still half-wrapped in a towel. He seems glad to be safe and warm.

You and Neely sit quietly for a moment, not quite sure what to say after such a dramatic rescue. Finally, Neely asks, "Are you ready to give Pepper back now?"

You sigh wearily.

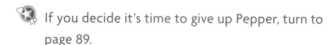 If you decide it's time to give up Pepper, turn to page 89.

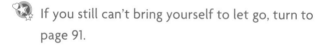 If you still can't bring yourself to let go, turn to page 91.

Amber appreciates your willingness to do whatever needs to be done on Parents' Day. After talking with the manager, Amber puts you in charge of greeting customers at the door. It's not as much fun as working with animals, but that's okay. You're just glad to be able to help out.

When Mrs. Thompson walks in with Pepper, your heart leaps. Pepper gives you a warm welcome. You meet Mrs. Thompson's daughter, too, a sandy-haired girl a little younger than you. You never knew Pepper had a girl of his own. You're a little jealous, but also glad that Pepper is back with his family, who must have missed him terribly.

Mrs. Thompson asks if she can sign up Pepper for obedience training. "I'm hoping that training will help him learn to stay put," she says, sounding a little embarrassed. "We all know Pepper has a problem with that!"

You laugh nervously, thinking that Mrs. Thompson doesn't know the half of it. But when you see how loving she is with Pepper, you make up your mind that someday soon, you'll tell her the whole truth.

You're relieved that Pepper will finally get training to keep him safe. You should've trusted that Amber would make sure of that. You give Pepper a quick hug, and then send him and his people out to the play yard to join the other families and the dogs they love.

The End

Amber lets you leave a little early. When you get back to your room, Pepper is whining to go out. You decide to take him somewhere he can really run and play—the beach.

As you walk toward the lake, you spot a couple of girls riding bikes. You try to keep your distance, but Pepper has other ideas. He bolts toward the bikes, and the leash slips out of your hand.

Pepper runs in front of the bikes, barking wildly. You scream, and so do the bikers. One swerves and tumbles off her bike onto the path in front of the library.

Turn to page 90.

Amber says that the center could still use your help on Parents' Day, but she has one condition for you—that you apologize to the Thompsons. You don't know how to face them, so you write a letter. It's hard to do, but you feel much better after you send the letter.

You help Isabel make bandannas for the pups, and on Parents' Day, she surprises you with a blue bandanna of your own—one to match Pepper's. You're about to put it on when you see Mrs. Thompson walking up with a young girl beside her. You fight the urge to run and hide. Instead, you take a deep breath and greet them.

Mrs. Thompson says, "I wanted to thank you for your letter. I know it was probably tough to write."

You nod, feeling your cheeks burn.

"This is my daughter, Chloe," Mrs. Thompson adds, looking down at the girl beside her. Chloe must be upset with you, because she won't meet your eyes. She fiddles with the bandanna around Pepper's neck.

That gives you an idea. You hold out your own blue bandanna toward Chloe, glancing at Isabel for permission. She nods. Then you say, "Here, this is for you."

Chloe looks up, surprised. She thanks you for the bandanna, and you help her put it on.

As the Thompsons walk away, you feel sadness, yet relief. Pepper is home safe with his family—a family who obviously loves him. *That's* what matters most.

The End

You look at Pepper, who is already falling asleep. The swimming has finally worn him out—for now. It's clear to you that you can't keep this energetic pup. "But how can I protect Pepper if I don't keep watch over him?" you ask Neely sadly.

"I don't know," Neely answers. "But maybe Amber will. Do you want me to go with you to find her?"

You nod. You can't speak; there's a lump in your throat. You gently wake up Pepper and clip on his leash.

The walk to Pet-Palooza is the longest walk of your life. You find Amber in the kitty cuddling area with a caramel-colored cat nestled in her lap. Amber is ecstatic to see Pepper, until she hears what you have to say. Then she gets super serious.

"We'll talk later," Amber says. "Right now, I have to get Pepper back to his owner." *His owner.* The words hurt.

Neely is waiting for you just outside Pet-Palooza. You don't talk much on the walk home, but you're sure thankful to have such a kind and loyal friend by your side.

 Turn to page 92.

You race toward the biker, hoping she's okay. You're relieved to find that she is. She's just a little shocked and embarrassed.

"You should keep a better eye on your dog," says the other biker, irritated.

Funny, you think. That's exactly what you wanted to say to the Thompsons—until you realized just how hard it is to keep track of a husky pup. There's no time to dwell on that thought now, though, because you have to chase down Pepper.

You're pretty sure he ran toward Five-Points Plaza. Sure enough, you spot him standing on the edge of the fountain, lapping at the water.

When Pepper sees you, his ears perk up and his body stiffens. No doubt, he's preparing for another chase. You talk in a gentle voice, trying to calm him down while you figure out a plan.

 If you run directly toward Pepper, turn to page 97.

 If you walk around the fountain to catch him off-guard, turn to page 98.

Pepper is still a little wet from his adventure in the lake. He's chewing happily on his rubber bone.

"I can't give him back," you say to Neely. "As hard as it is to take care of a puppy, I have to try to protect Pepper."

A shadow of concern falls across Neely's face. She turns away from you.

"Are you going to tell?" you ask her.

Neely shrugs. "I don't know what to do," she admits. "I have to think about it."

Neely gets up to leave. She offers you a sad smile on her way out the door.

You want to swear Neely to secrecy, to beg for her loyalty, but you can't. All you can do is hope that she gives you enough time to figure out a way to help Pepper.

 Turn to page 93.

You show up for your Pet-Palooza shift on Tuesday. You don't know what else to do. Amber seems disappointed in you. You can tell because she doesn't chat with you about the weekend or fill you in on any funny stories about the animals she has cared for recently. She just asks you to put some files in order.

While you're filing, Amber stocks shelves. Out of the blue, she says matter-of-factly, "You did the right thing by bringing Pepper back." At the mention of Pepper's name, you start to cry. You really miss him.

Amber's voice softens. "Do you want to have that talk now?" she asks.

"Sounds good," you say meekly. Your legs feel like wobbly rubber as you follow Amber into the empty pet-sitter classroom. You sit next to her on a folding chair.

Amber sighs, as if this is hard for her, too. "I know you care a lot about animals," she says. "That's good, because there are lots of them who need your love and care."

You nod. You're still too sad to speak.

"How about if you take time off from the center to think about ways to raise money for the animal shelter in town?" Amber asks. She smiles and touches your hand. "It'll take your mind off Pepper, and help other animals, too."

You take a deep breath and say, "Okay."

 Turn to page 76.

On Monday morning, you're ten minutes late to math class because Pepper takes forever to do his business outside. You also miss breakfast. It's hard to concentrate on an empty stomach. You spend the hour worrying about Pepper and listening to your stomach rumble.

When you get back to your room after class, Pepper is gone! How could he have gotten out with the door closed? You look everywhere, even outside in the woods around Brightstar House and over by the lake. You pass a bunch of girls, but you can't exactly ask them if they've seen the dog from the "missing" poster.

There's no trace of Pepper. You're frantic, and it suddenly hits you that this is *exactly* how the Thompsons must feel.

 Turn to page 77.

Pepper is loving the chase! He keeps turning around to make sure you and Neely are behind him, and then he bursts on ahead. Now he's sprinting toward Starfire Lake.

Pepper slows down when he reaches the lakeshore. He darts in and out of the tall grass, chasing something you can't see. You're almost close enough to grab him, until he spots something in the water and starts barking wildly. Two ducks are swimming near shore. With dismay, you watch Pepper hit the water with a splash and start dog-paddling toward them. "Pepper, no!" you yell.

As you wade into the water after Pepper, Neely calls you back to shore. "Wait!" she cries. "You don't know how deep it is!"

You ignore Neely. You're too worried about Pepper. As the pup swims out farther, following the ducks, they get nervous. They quack and fly out of the water with a terrific splash. When they're gone, Pepper starts swimming in circles, wondering where they went.

You're in up to your waist now, and the lake mud is sucking at your feet. "Here, Pepper, I'm over here," you call in a gentle voice. This time, Pepper listens. He turns around and paddles toward you. When he reaches you, the tired pup tries to climb up on your shoulders. You wrap your arms around him and wade back toward shore.

 Turn to page 84.

You say, "I hope I can still help out with the fund-raising event—to make up for what I did." Amber doesn't say no, so you keep on going. "What if we have a Dog Jog?" you ask her. "People could sign up to run a mile or two with their pets and raise money for the animal shelter."

Amber smiles. "I guess I don't have to ask how you came up with that idea!" she says.

You giggle. You're still calming down from your own "jog" with Pepper, who is finally snuggled next to you, asleep.

Amber's expression turns serious. "I'll ask the manager about a Dog Jog," she says, "but before you start planning the event, there's something you should probably do."

"Apologize to the Thompsons?" you ask, pretty much knowing the answer.

Amber nods. Then she says, "I'll talk to them about getting Pepper some good training. Maybe we can teach him how to 'stay' after all."

You share a moment of silent understanding. You're grateful for Amber's support and loyalty. Apologizing to the Thompsons will be hard, but you can do it. It'll be the first step toward making things right.

The End

When Pepper sees you running after him, he leaps down happily from the edge of the fountain and races across the plaza.

"Pepper, stop!" you call out in frustration.

Pepper heads all the way through the plaza and out the other side. He's on the path that leads to the far corner of campus. The only thing there is the Good Sports Center. You tense up. If a game is going on at the center, there'll be a crowd of people there, and you'll never find Pepper. You quicken your pace.

There's a fence running around the edge of the sports center. The gate is wide open, and you can hear shouts and cheers coming from inside. Uh-oh. Pepper, who loves people and action, heads right through the gate and disappears into a sea of people.

 Turn to page 106.

You wait until Pepper looks away, and then you walk slowly around the other side of the fountain to catch him off-guard. As you get closer, you think you've got him. But he suddenly spots you. His tail starts to wag. He still thinks you're playing a game.

As you take one more step toward Pepper, he darts away from you. He zips down the side path away from the plaza and toward the shops on the edge of campus.

"Pepper!" you wail as you take off after him. By this point, your lungs are burning. Your plan hasn't worked out quite the way you'd hoped it would.

Suddenly, you have a hunch as to where Pepper is going. Pet-Palooza is in the shopping area, and Pepper has never had trouble finding his way there. You set out for the pet-care center. Amber may be there, and you're terrified of facing her right now. But you're even more scared of losing Pepper.

 Turn to page 109.

You skip lunch, trying to avoid Neely—and everyone else. But after lunch, someone knocks on your door.

It's Neely. "I know you're angry," she says, "but I want you to know that I kept your secret. I had to return Pepper, but I did it for you, too. A loyal friend tries to keep her friends out of trouble."

Neely's freckled face is full of sincerity. She's trying to make things better, but all you want to do right now is run away. You decide you need a walk to clear your head.

If you tell Neely that you want to walk alone, turn to page 100.

If you let her come with you, turn to page 102.

A loyal friend tries to keep her friends out of trouble.

You walk all the way around the lake and then up to the Student Center. You're suddenly starving. It's too late to get lunch, so you head to the bakery for dessert.

Logan is behind the counter sliding a batch of cookies onto a plate. "I'll take two," you say to her over the counter.

Logan laughs. "These are canine cookies for the fund-raiser," she says. "They're made out of baby food and wheat germ."

DRINKS

Pink lemonade	$1.50
Iced tea	$1.50
Chocolate milk	$1.50
Vanilla shake	$2.50
Berry smoothie	$2.75
Peppermint tea	$1.25
Hot chocolate	$1.50
Café mocha	$2.50
Caramel latte	$2.75
Chai tea latte	$2.50

"...walk your dog
today."

I give your
dog a treat!

3. A dog is a
girl's best
friend! ☺

"Yum," you joke. You're not so hungry anymore.

You decide to stay and visit with Logan for a while. It's nice to talk with someone who doesn't work at Pet-Palooza or know Pepper. You don't tell Logan everything, but you do tell her that a good friend of yours betrayed your trust.

 Turn to page 104.

BAKED GOODS

Cookie	$ .50
Cupcake	$1.00
Brownie	$ .75
Muffin	$1.25
Cake	$2.50
Cheesecake	$2.75

You and Neely are walking side by side, yet it feels as if you are miles apart. As you walk along the lakeshore, your anger starts to cool. You know that Neely feels bad that she upset you, and that she is on your side.

"You were trying to help me do the right thing," you finally admit. "But I'm really going to miss Pepper. What am I going to do now?"

Neely thinks for a while. "Maybe," she says, "you can focus on the fund-raiser. Pepper has a home, but think of all the other animals who need one."

Neely has a good point. It breaks your heart to think of those animals, some of whom were abandoned by their owners. The thought makes you realize, again, that the Thompsons aren't bad owners. They could be a lot worse.

Neely picks up a leaf and twirls it. She hands it to you as a funny peace offering. "Hey!" she exclaims suddenly. "Want to help me with the animal sketches I'm making for the fund-raiser?"

You frown. "My scribbles next to yours?" you say. "Not a pretty picture." This makes you both laugh. But you *would* like to do something for the fund-raiser.

⭐ If you tell Neely that you'll find a way to help her with her sketches, turn to page 105.

⭐ If you tell her "No, thanks," that you're thinking up an idea of your own, turn to page 76.

You sit in the grass a while longer. You're really tired. It was a lot of work to care for Pepper in your room, and a lot of work to tell the truth about it. It must have been hard for Isabel to be a good friend to you through all of this, too.

Then you think of Pepper. It was painful to say good-bye to him. You picture him with his owners, and you feel a twinge of jealousy, but also relief. Pepper is with people he loves, who seem to love him an awful lot, too.

You remind yourself that you'll see Pepper again. At least you hope you will. But you're going to have to work extra hard to earn back Amber's trust before she'll let you work at Pet-Palooza again.

You think of all the ways you can try to make things up to Amber and to Isabel, like helping Amber clean puppy kennels and helping Isabel with her bandannas for the fund-raiser. But first you need a really long nap. You stand up, brush yourself off, and head for home.

The End

"Why would a friend betray you?" Logan asks.

You never thought to ask that question, but Logan would—she's curious about everything. You try to explain it to her. "Well," you say, "she thought she was doing the right thing. She was worried about me. She didn't actually tell my secret. She just . . ."

You trail off, and Logan looks confused. "But a girl who looks out for you sounds like a pretty good friend," she says.

You feel your stomach twist. "Yeah," you say. "Yeah, I guess she is." You tell Logan that you have to go.

 If you go see Neely, turn to page 108.

 If you go to Pet-Palooza, turn to page 112.

A girl who looks out for you is a pretty good friend.

You tell Neely that if she sketches the animal pictures, you'll frame them. The two of you put your heads together to come up with an interesting way to decorate the frames. First, you paint the frames in bright colors, like pink and yellow. Then you use black ink to make thumbprints all around the edges. After that, you add three dots to each print so that the thumbprints look like puppy paw prints.

Working together is good for you and Neely. Things start to feel normal between you two again. And when the frames are done, boy are they cute! You know they'll sell well.

The day of the fund-raiser, Neely gives you a gift. It's a framed picture that she drew of you and Pepper. You know it's her way of helping you feel better, and it does the trick. You're truly touched.

You give Neely a big hug and say, "I know you know how much Pepper means to me. But do you know how much *you* mean to me?"

Neely blushes with embarrassment, but you can tell that she's pleased. You study the picture of Pepper again and smile, grateful for your two good friends.

The End

The game is in full swing. You see Riley on the field. Suddenly the crowd goes wild—cheering and pointing. There's Pepper, racing down the field toward the ball!

The whistle blows, and all the players start running after Pepper. He jumps and barks and races in circles. You step onto the field and call to him. When Riley sees you, she rushes over. "Is that the lost dog?" she asks you.

"Yeah, I've been chasing him," you say, out of breath. "He sees this as a big game, and he's definitely winning."

Riley laughs. "The best way to get dogs to come is to run *away* from them, not toward them," she says.

"Good tip!" you say. You run out onto the field. As you jog past Pepper, you call his name. He perks up his ears and then starts racing after you. It's working!

  Turn to page 113.

Neely opens her door on the first knock. She looks really relieved to see you.

"I'm sorry," you say right away. "I'm sorry that I put you in a bad spot and that I—"

Neely hugs you before you can even get all the words out. "It's okay," she says. "You were in a bad spot, too."

Neely invites you in to hang out and talk some more. You take her up on it. There's still a lot left for you to face: going back to Pet-Palooza, seeing Pepper and the Thompsons again, and maybe telling Amber what really happened to Pepper. But with a loyal friend beside you— a friend who will help you do the right thing—you know you'll be okay.

The End

When you get to Pet-Palooza, though, Pepper isn't waiting outside the door like you thought he'd be. You check the play area across the street. No sign of Pepper there, either, but a poodle barks you a greeting through the gate.

You rush inside Pet-Palooza. Breathlessly, you ask a new volunteer if she has seen a gray and white husky pup running around the center.

"Nope, sorry," she answers. She starts dialing a number on the phone but then quickly hangs up. "Whoa, you don't mean that lost dog, do you?" she asks with wide, worried eyes.

Amber must have heard you two talking, because she pokes her head into the lobby and asks you what's going on. You're still out of breath, and still afraid to tell Amber the truth. You think about telling her that you're just out for a morning jog. The thing is, though, you need her help. So you say, "I spotted Pepper. I think he's in this area."

That's all Amber needs to hear. She grabs a leash and follows you right out the door.

 Turn to page 111.

You decide that rather than wait till Parents' Day to raise money for the local animal shelter, you'll start right now. You decorate a box to look like a doghouse. It even has a picture of a puppy with floppy ears looking out the window.

You take your box door-to-door at Brightstar House asking girls for donations for the shelter. "Even twenty-five cents will keep a precious pup off the street and fed for a day," you say.

The first person to donate is Isabel, who gives you five whole dollars! "To get you off to a roaring start," she says.

The second donation comes from Neely, who says, "Good job. You're really inspiring me to help a charity."

After that, you feel confident enough to ask everyone in Brightstar House. Most girls love animals as much as you do, so your box grows heavy with change and bills.

You can't wait to see Amber's face when you bring the money to her on Parents' Day. You're doing something great for local animals, and you hope you'll be repairing a friendship, too.

The End

"Let's split up," Amber suggests. "You head that way, and I'll head this way."

"Good idea. Hopefully we'll corner him," you call back as you start to jog. Your heart pounds, as it did the first time you knew Pepper was running loose in such a busy area. You try to calm down. You need all of your senses to find Pepper. You steady your breathing and strain your ears for any sounds that might lead you to Pepper.

There it is! You hear an excited yipping up ahead. *Don't celebrate yet*, you warn yourself. It could be any dog. But as you jog down the path toward the Market, you see Pepper dancing around two people. You warm with relief, until you look closer. You freeze.

It's Mrs. Thompson. She's standing beside a pretty girl with sandy curls, who must be her daughter. Your stomach drops. You watch for a while as Pepper plasters the young girl with kisses. The girl is clearly just as happy to see Pepper. She bursts into tears of relief and wraps her arms around Pepper's neck.

If you walk toward Mrs. Thompson and her daughter, turn to page 114.

If you walk the other way, hoping you won't be seen, turn to page 116.

"I'll take one of those canine cookies after all—for a friend," you tell Logan. "Oh, and a human cookie, too!" You pay Logan, and she wraps up the goodies in little bags.

As you walk toward Pet-Palooza, you plan your words carefully. You need to take responsibility for what you did and prove that you really do want what's best for Pepper.

You pat the cookies in your pocket—a canine cookie for Pepper and a chocolate-chip cookie you'll give to Neely later. You know now that you put Neely in a really tough spot. She had to lie to Amber to protect you.

You also know that the best way to make things up to Neely is to tell Amber the truth. She may ban you from working at Pet-Palooza for a while, but you can handle that. You're tired of the lies and the secrets, and you're ready to be a good friend again—to Neely, to Amber, *and* to Pepper.

The End

The crowd applauds as you run out of the Good Sports Center with Pepper close behind. Instead of heading back toward Five-Points Plaza, you find yourself running in the other direction—toward Pet-Palooza. Your legs seem to have made up their mind for you.

You burst through the doors of Pet-Palooza with Pepper on your heels. When he realizes where he is, he yips excitedly and leaps up and down around your legs.

Amber comes out of the back room, wondering what all the fuss is about. When she sees Pepper, she starts jumping up and down, too. "You found him!" she says, giving you a huge hug.

But now that you've stopped running, you can't catch your breath. You're relieved and exhausted and embarrassed all at once, and you start to cry.

Amber stops smiling. "What is it?" she asks. "What's wrong?"

 Turn to page 115.

When Mrs. Thompson sees you, you think she's going to hug you. "Thank you, thank you!" she keeps repeating. She must think that you're the one who found Pepper.

When Amber runs up to join you, Mrs. Thompson gushes about how heroic you were. You don't know what to say. Amber seems to sense your discomfort, because she says, "Let's go back to Pet-Palooza and give Pepper a quick checkup, and maybe some food and water."

"Want to come?" asks Mrs. Thompson's daughter, giving you a shy grin.

"Um, no, but thanks," you say awkwardly. What you really want to do is get out of here. You walk with everyone to Pet-Palooza, just to be polite. But then you say that you have to go.

You take one last look at Pepper as he disappears through the door of Pet-Palooza. He doesn't turn around to see if you're following him, which hurts a little. But what matters most now is that Pepper is back with his family, and he's happy. You have a feeling that you won't be happy anytime soon—especially after you tell Amber the truth about what happened. Sighing deeply, you set off on the path toward home.

The End

You sit down on the floor next to Pepper, who licks away your tears. That makes you feel better. "Thanks, Pepper," you whisper, stroking his head.

You take a deep breath and tell Amber the truth—that you didn't find Pepper. "I'm the one who hid him," you admit. "I thought I was protecting him from getting hurt, from running away again. But then . . ." You shake your head and tell Amber about the mad chase across campus.

To your surprise, Amber half-smiles. She sits down on the floor beside you. "So, you didn't do so well with training Pepper not to run away?" she asks, grinning more broadly now.

"Uh, no, obviously not," you say. You can't help smiling, too. "If I hadn't been so scared for Pepper, the whole thing might have been kind of funny," you tell Amber.

Even Pepper seems to be smiling now. "You had fun anyway, didn't you, boy?" you say to him. And that gives you an idea—two ideas, actually. "Hey!" you say to Amber. "I just thought of some things we could do for the Pet-Palooza fund-raiser."

"Really?" says Amber, looking at you with curiosity. "Care to share?"

 If you share your idea for a "Fun with Dogs" field day, turn to page 119.

 If you share your idea for a "Dog Jog," turn to page 96.

★ 116 ★

You're walking away when Pepper catches sight—or scent—of you. He bounds toward you, barking. *There's no sneaking away from this pup,* you think sadly.

When you reach down to grab Pepper's leash, he takes off running in the other direction, back toward the Thompsons. He runs back and forth, as if he's torn. But for the first time in days, you're not.

You thought the Thompsons were neglectful owners, but you know better now. If they were, Pepper wouldn't be so happy to see them. Plus, you think about all of the times Pepper raced off while you were watching him. You couldn't control Pepper any more than the Thompsons could. The next time Pepper races your way, you nab his leash and lead him back to the Thompsons.

You attempt a smile as you approach the sandy-haired girl. "I'm glad you found Pepper—or that he found you," you say in a quivery voice.

After an embarrassing round of thank-yous, the Thompsons lead Pepper away. You want to run after him, but you keep walking in the other direction. You have to— it's the right thing to do, even though it hurts.

 Turn to page 118.

★ 118 ★

Amber is running down the path toward you, calling your name. When she gets close enough to see the look on your face, her brown eyes fill with worry. "What is it?" she asks. You don't answer her. You can't speak over the lump in your throat.

Amber puts a protective arm around you. "Do you want to go back to Pet-Palooza and talk?" she asks.

All you can do is nod. You find a place to sit in the grassy play area across from Pet-Palooza. Then you blurt out everything, starting with how you found Pepper and ending with how much you learned from your mistakes.

"You kept Pepper for two days?" Amber asks. You're sure she's going to scold you, but she doesn't. "You know, then, how hard it is to take care of a pup," she says, "and how scary it is to lose your pet and not know where he is."

You nod miserably. Amber must know that you learned your lesson, because she doesn't say anything more. But when she goes back into Pet-Palooza, she doesn't ask you to come with her.

Turn to page 103.

You plunge in. "How about a 'Fun with Dogs' field day at the Good Sports Center? Pepper sure had fun on the soccer field," you add with a laugh. "Dog owners could bring their dogs to the sports center and pay to play games with them, like kicking them soccer balls—"

"Or tossing tennis balls," Amber adds. She's getting caught up in the idea now, too.

You nod eagerly. "All the money could be donated to the animal shelter. And Pepper would love to play games all day. It would be so much fun to have him there." You're silent for a moment, realizing that to have Pepper there, you'll need to do something first. "Amber," you say softly, "I need to apologize to the Thompsons."

Amber nods and says, "That sounds like a good idea. And when you're done talking to the Thompsons, I'll talk with them about getting Pepper enrolled in obedience training. If he can be taught to 'stay,' he'll be much safer."

That makes you feel better. And thinking about your fund-raising ideas makes you happier than you've felt in days. You decide to ask Riley to help. You bet she's never coached puppies on the soccer field before, but you're pretty sure she'll say yes!

The End